This book belongs to

....

....

....

....

This is a Bright Sparks Book.
First published 2000
Bright Sparks
Queen Street House,
4, Queen Street,
Bath, BA1 1HE, UK.
Copyright © Parragon 2000

Produced for Parragon Books by
Oyster Books Ltd, Unit 4, Kirklea Farm,
Badgworth, Somerset, BS26 2QH, UK

Illustrated by Andrew Geeson
Written by Marilyn Tolhurst

Printed in Italy

ISBN 1 84250 063 5

A WINDY DAY

Illustrated by Andrew Geeson

Bright ☆ Sparks

It was a bright and breezy morning at Faraway Farm. Rosie looked out of her bedroom window.

"Come and look Mum," she called. "The clouds are like big fluffy sheep running across blue grass."

"Mmm, it looks like a good day for hanging out the washing," said Mum. "It will soon dry in a breeze like this"

Rosie and Danny helped Mum sort out all the washing. There were sheets and towels, shirts and socks, Danny's muddy football jersey, Rosie's best party dress....

...Dad's stripey jumper and the yellow spotty rug that Conker the dog slept on.

"Billy the rabbit needs a bath," said Rosie. "His ears are dirty and he's spilt cocoa all down his jacket."

"It was you that spilt cocoa down his jacket," laughed Danny.

"I only asked him if he wanted a little sip," replied Rosie.

Mum put on the radio and sang along with the music. Rosie put in the washing powder and Danny turned on the knobs. Conker got under everyone's feet and Stan the cat, kept trying to sleep in the washing basket.

The last thing to go in was Billy the rabbit.

The washing was soon done. Mum carried the basket full of heavy wet clothes. Rosie carried Billy. He was now beautifully clean but dripping wet.

"We'll hang Billy on the line, too" said Mum. "He'll be dry in no time!"

When they went outside, the wind was blowing hard. Joe, the farm worker, was trying to mend the gate and hold on to his hat at the same time!

"Ooh, look at the cloud sheep," cried Rosie. "They are really running fast now!"

"I should peg that washing on tight if I were you," shouted Joe. "The wind is getting stronger and stronger. Mick can't get his milk lorry through because there's a fallen tree across the road."

The sheets billowed like the sails of a ship, the socks bounced up and down and Dad's stripey jumper looked like it had somebody inside it. Danny spread his arms wide and ran around the yard pretending to be an aeroplane.

"Whee! I love windy days!", he cried
"Billy the rabbit is dancing on the line," exclaimed Rosie.
"Come on. Inside, you two" ordered Mum.

The wind got stronger and stronger. It rattled the windows and made whistling noises under the door.

"Look, here comes Jack!" cried Rosie. "Oops! The wind has blown off his hat!"

"Oh dear," said Mum. "I think we had better check the washing".

Whoooosh! The wind nearly knocked them over when they went outside.

"Help! I'm being blown awaaaay," shouted Rosie.

"So are all Jack's letters. Look. They are all over the lane," said Danny.

"Mum!" gasped Danny. "Where's the washing's gone? Where's my football jersey?"

"Where's my Billy?" wailed Rosie.

There were sheets in the hedges, socks in the duck pond and letters all over the lane. Dad's stripey jumper was halfway up the apple tree.

"Here's my football jersey," shouted Danny. "It's muddier than when I played in it."

Conker found his spotty rug and sat down on it to stop it blowing in with the chickens.

"Well, that's about the lot," said Mum. "Quick let's take it inside before the wind gets it again."

"It looks like Jack found all his letters," said Danny

"But where's my Billy?" sobbed Rosie.

"Come and look at this," called Joe. "The little piglets have found a new friend."

Right in the middle of the pig pen sat Billy the rabbit. The piglets were squealing with excitement and twirling their curly tails.

"Oh there you are, you blow-away rabbit," smiled Rosie. "I know the piglets are very friendly but now you've got mud all over your jacket. You are a silly Billy. I'll have to give you a bath all over again."